The Silent Life Within
Readings for Writers Volume 3

Mike Smith

Copyright © 2016 Mike Smith

All rights reserved.

ISBN:1537388541
ISBN-13:9781537388540

PREFACE

In this third collection of essays on short stories and their writers, I take a look at the Gainsborough adaptations of Somerset Maugham's short stories, and compare three tales – by Pritchett, Bates and Mansfield – that share some common themes. There are stories by H.G.Wells and Sir Arthur Quiller-Couch, alongside examples by Mrs W.K.Clifford (aka Lucy Lane Clifford), Mary Mann, Daphne Du Maurier and Elizabeth Taylor. George Moore's acclaimed collection, *The Untilled Field* comes under scrutiny and provides my volume title, and there is a story of the Siege of Paris from Alphonse Daudet (in translation). To complete the dozen, there is a tale of the Battle of the Sexes from the early 18thC by Justus Van Effen, and, from a 2014 Fiction Desk anthology, a type of ghost story by Matt Plass.

CONTENTS

Acknowledgments

1	The Magic Shop (H.G.Well)	1
2	Little Brother (Mary Mann)	10
3	The Untilled Field (George Moore)	18
4	Belisaire's Prussion (Alphonse Daudet)	32
5	How To Cure A Fussy Wife (Justus van Effen)	40
6	Fellow Travellers: Pritchett, Bates & Mansfield	46
7	Next to Godliness (Matt Plass)	56
8	The Blush (Elizabeth Taylor)	62
9	Somerset Maugham Adapted	66
10	The Heart of the Wood (Mrs W.K.Clifford)	74
11	Captain Knott (Sir Arthur Quiller-Couch)	82
12	Built Upon Deceit (Daphne Du Maurier's The Old Man)	87

ACKNOWLEDGMENTS

Built Upon Deceit has appeared on *Thresholds*, website of The International Short Story Forum, along with an earlier version of *Somerset Maugham Adapted*.

1 THE MAGIC SHOP BY H.G.WELLS

In H.G.Wells' story, *The Magic Shop*, a boy and his father visit the eponymous emporium, and are shown tricks and sleights of hand that become progressively more fantastic, until excitement turns to terror.

Not so much a tale about a boy, or even about a parent and a boy, it is an exploration of the experience of being a parent. First published in 1903 (according to Wickipedia) it has a light, humorous tone, without the apocalyptic darkness of many other works. Wells foresaw, and lived through two World Wars, but this piece of magic realism seems unclouded by that vision. It is a delightful foray into a world of unbridled imagination that first pin-pricks, and then shreds the bubble of rational thought. The protagonists, and especially the father, who narrates the tale, are taken on a journey that is beyond their control right from the start, and which ends with a jolt, leaving the narrator to ponder, and doubt, and to recognise the developing separation between him and his son, Gip.

It is also a writers' tale, in that it is one about the meaning of words, and the way we use them and understand them: where metaphor and literality become blurred.

That blurring begins before the two have even entered the shop, which the narrator has seen, but which Gip 'hauled me by my finger' to.

> 'I had not thought the place was there..........
> I had fancied it was down nearer the Circus, or round the corner in Oxford Street,'

'Fancied' is the right word, and though there's no doubt we're in London, we're already, to a certain extent, lost. There is 'something of the mirage' already present.

Using a technique that runs all the way through the story, Wells has his narrator tell us the simple truth, which, of course, can mean two completely different things.

> 'It was no common shop this; it was a magic shop,'

And within it, magic is what they are shown. Even the arrival of the shop assistant is fraught with ambiguity, and doubt.

'...the shopman, as I suppose, came in.'

And again:

'.....spreading his magic fingers on the glass case.'

Whatever he is, the 'shopman' gets off to a magic start.

'Then, quite distinctly, he drew from his head a glass ball.'

The parent is willing to enter into the spirit. Has he not seen the trick 'endless times before'?

'"That's good," I said, with a laugh.'

But when Gip reaches out for the ball, "It's in your pocket," the shopman tells him, and, magically, it is! Remarkably, it's also free. And the shopman produces several more to go with it. There's a subtle change in the parental response then.

'I laughed in the manner of one who subscribes to a jest.'

The shopman produces a business card, and points out the word 'Genuine' printed upon it. He says, with absolute sincerity, what we would, if we weren't reading this story, take for a permissible falsehood:

'There is absolutely no deception, sir.'

Our narrator's unease grows slightly, and more so, when the shopman tells Gip he is 'the Right Sort of Boy.' This cuts the heart of the relationship between Gip and his father, because it is exactly what the father believes too, and I see this as Wells pushing the shopman in between the two of them for the first time. The narrator is surprised 'at his knowing that,' which suggests both that intimacy has been invaded, and that it is true.

'..we keep it rather a secret at home.'

That the shopman should know such secrets is perhaps more alarming than that he should perform such magic tricks as we have already seen. But the magic is part of the shop too, for at that moment a different sort of boy tries to get in, but the shop door is locked against him. They hear the boy and his father rattling the door.

'"It's locked, Edward," he said.

"But it isn't," I said

"It is sir," said the shopman, "always -for that sort of child."

It's not what the narrator says next, but what he does, that shows how the tension has been heightened.

'...I said, breathing a little more freely.'

From this point on the shopman seems freed of all restraint.

The tricks become wilder. The shopman himself becomes, well, almost magical.

'...he really had an extraordinarily long body'

But the magic seems catching too.

'With a start, I discovered something moving about in my hat,'

The shopman, pulls out a pigeon, a marble, a watch and more glass balls, and then reams of paper.

'All sorts of things accumulate, sir.'

He vanishes behind the growing mound of paper, and then, with a particularly enjoyable image – which I can't help thinking must reflect a feeling that Wells expects us all to know, and to share, even if we have not acted upon it – his voice ceases.

'...exactly like when you hit a neighbour's gramophone with a well-aimed brick, the same instant silence,..'

The shopman has vanished, but there are more disconcerting issues. Though Gip is having a wonderful time, his father has noticed something that he keeps to himself.

'...if the counter wouldn't suddenly extend itself to shut one off from the door.'

Equally, perhaps more alarmingly, a door appears, and suddenly they are being shown into the 'show-room,' and the parent's fears are articulated, quite explicitly, for the first time.

'I was beginning to think the magic just a little too genuine.'

Then the first truly sinister magic happens, for the shopman, who has reappeared, 'rubbing his flexible hands together,' reaches out.

'I felt him pull at something that clung to my coat sleeve, and then I saw he held a little, wriggling red demon by the tail....'

More frightening, to the parent, is that Gip lets go of his father's finger, and has passed into the control of the shopman.

'He had got Gip now; he had got him away from my finger;'

This is the real fear of the magic: that the boy is passing from his father's influence to that of the outsider, to that of the outside world, and the parent is powerless to prevent it. The man teaches Gip a magic word, which the parent cannot quite grasp, but Gip hears it, and can use it right away, to bring a box of toy soldiers to life.

"I myself haven't a very quick ear and it was a tongue twisting sound, but Gip-he has his mother's ear-'

This slipping away from us is what growing up is all about.

That our children are not our own is what, I think, this story is all about. The shopman says again, quite plainly, and this time we don't take it for metaphor:

'"This is the genuine magic," he said. "The real thing."'

Then, while the parent follows them, almost in a daze, the shopman brings Gip to a place where Gip, on a stool, 'thinking no evil' has 'a sort of big drum' popped over his head. The father sees the game, but is too late to stop it, and again, what he says reminds us that this story is about the magic of words too.

"Take that off," I cried, "this instant. You'll frighten the boy...'

But we know that it is not the boy who is frightened, only the parent. And it seems with good cause, for when the drum is taken off, the stool is empty. Gip has vanished. There is then a description of what it feels like when a 'sinister something.....grips your heart' and Wells' narrator demands, impotently, the return of his child.

'"Stop!" I said, and he laughed, receding. I leapt after him- into utter darkness.'

This is not the end of the story. Far from it. There is the best part of two pages still to go. The leap has carried our man out onto

Regent Street again, and Gip is with him. The magic shop has disappeared. What can they do, but take a cab, and return home, Gip clutching four parcels.

'He looked completely undamaged.'

And his father has an insight, that we might find a little dated, though many, I suspect, will not.

> '..for a moment I was sorry I was his father and not his mother, and so couldn't suddenly there, *coram public,* in our hansom, kiss him.'

The parcels contain three boxes of 'quite ordinary lead soldiers,' and a living kitten, which 'had only the magic natural to all kittens.' The father is relieved, but changed. He hangs 'about in the nursery for quite an unconscionable time...' Time passes, but one day he ventures to ask a question of Gip.

'"How would you like your soldiers to come alive, Gip...?'

To which Gip replies:

'"Mine do."'

The narrator finishes his story on the 'question of finance.' He is used to paying his bills, but cannot find the shop again. He reasons that, 'whoever they may be' will 'send in their bill in their own time.'

It seems, perhaps, a curious place to end, but it does echo something the shopman has said, right at the start of the adventure, when he was explaining that the glass balls were always free.

'Though we pay in the end. But not so heavily-as people suppose...'

Perhaps he was talking about parenthood. Perhaps the father has, after all, already paid his dues.

2 LITTLE BROTHER
BY MARY MANN

Mary Mann's (1862-1929) four-page short story, coming in at just under fifteen hundred words, is one of a disappointingly few really good stories to be found in A.S.Byatt's bewildering gathering for the *Oxford Book of English Short Stories*.

It is, Byatt tells us, a 'grim little Norfolk tale of rural poverty,' and if that were all it was, I suppose it would still fit the brief of the collection. Later in her introduction Byatt contrasts Mann with near contemporary, Ronald Firbank, who she says is 'frivolous, brittle, delicious, and decadent' – Mann, presumably, being the opposite. In another reference, Byatt describes Mann's story as 'spiky with morals and the inadequacy of morals' and 'plain, and brief, and clear and terrible.' She also mentions the 'narrator's tone' as being 'not simple,' and all these little insights ring true.

Reminiscent of Coppard's rural tales – *The Poor Man* and *The Old Venerable* for example – and of Arthur Morrison's urban *Tales of Mean Streets*, the poverty is more starkly presented than the Norfolk. Not quite stereotypically, the Hodd family is large, ill kempt, and implicitly of the 'outsider' variety.

'...a wild unkempt-looking creature....a tangle of red hair.... Not such a family as the Hodds do we often see in Dulditch...'

The red hair, and one or two vowel sounds, suggest a Celtic, possibly Irish origin, and the comment about labour shortages would suggest an itinerant family – like the one in Coppard's *Weep Not My Wanton*.

'.....when we laves off wark.'

Yet the story implies also that the Hodds are firmly part of the village: the sort of family that would be visited by a 'better-spoken' neighbour!

[Hodd]'..always clears out on these occasions...'

The two ideas, in an English setting, are not mutually exclusive. The alien begins at the parish boundary, and persists until several generations of them have been buried in the local graveyard.

The story is simple, and a spoiler is unavoidable, for like *Weep Not My Wanton* it contains a startling revelation, which is not the point of the story. Mrs Hodd has given birth to her 13th child, but it is a still-birth, and the first person narrator visits the bed-ridden woman, to pay her respects. On the way he or she, we are not told and must make our own assumption, meets Hodd and his son, chopping turnips, in true Norfolk fashion. The conversation, and the description of Hodd and the boy add to our image of the family, and our expectations of Mrs Hodd.

> 'the little boy ……. also was red-headed, he also was attired for the most part in a sack…'

Hodd is avoiding his wife, and children:

> 'The place is chuck full of 'em. You stamp on 'em as you walk.'

Later, his wife tells us:

> 'Ah! Hodd, he han't a mother's heart'

In the lying in room, upstairs in the grubby cottage, the visitor asks to view the baby, and we discover that it is not lying on the makeshift bier. Mrs Hodd calls for her two youngest children, whom the visitor has already encountered, playing downstairs. She threatens retribution, but unless we've guessed, we know not what for.

> 'I'll warm yer jackets for ye when I git yer.'

The visitor offers to fetch them up, and goes down to where the two tots are playing with a battered doll.

> 'The tiny children on the filthy hearth were too much engrossed with their play to be aware of me...'

You may well have guessed, but in the story this is a slow reveal, hinted at several times before the suspected truth is confirmed. The doll is, in fact, the dead baby. It is not quite a case of 'Sarah Hall's Bung', but the surprise runs the risk of being tumbled to too easily, and Mann successfully distracts us. My first inkling came, not with the first appearance of the doll, nor with the request to see the baby, nor even with its absence from the bier, but with the word 'rigid', applied to the legs of the doll.

The language of the girl, playing with the doll, heightens both the suspicion, and the poignancy of the scene, for she is not rough, or unkind to her 'little brother.'

> 'Theer! Put ickle arms in! Put in ickle arms.'

The visitor confirms our fears, and were this the point of the story, it would have been the place to stop.

But the story does not stop. It goes on for a half a page or more. We are given more description of the playing, this time in the full knowledge of what is being played with.

> 'Evangeline and Randolph pushed their grubby fingers into the open mouth, and tried to force them into the sunken eyes...'

The visitor rescues the 'desecrated body' and returns to Mrs Hodd, whom she reproaches. This draws a response that closes the story, and gives it point.

'Other folkes' child'en have a toy, now and then, to kape 'em out o' mischief.'

The issue that Mrs Hodd raises is not new. It has been embedded in the story right from the beginning. From that comment spoken by the narrator to Hodd himself.

'They keep you poor I'm afraid.'

And Hodd's reply to it:

'There's no stoppin' my missus once she's got a-goin'.'

And to the one suppressed by the narrator:

'…it was hardly fair to put it all on to Mrs Hodd,'

The case has been made. Mrs Hodd too, has already commented on the feeding and clothing of her brood.

'If parson's folk want to see 'em clothed they must do it themselves. My job's their insides…'

It is inherent too, in the very opening of the story, where the nurse rushes from one birth to another.

'I met the parish nurse hurrying from the cottage in which a baby had been born, towards a cottage ......where a baby was due...'

This is a 'state of the nation' story, a term usually reserved for a type of novel.

Mary Mann's short story is interesting not only for its situation, and events, but for the narrative perspective. Not just the tone of the narrator, who speaks in standard English, but gives us the Hodd's possibly Norfolk dialect and accent, but more importantly because the arguments put forward to challenge the accepted wisdom of the both narrator, and implicitly, the reader, are put forward in the voice, not of that narrator, but of Mrs Hodd herself. She is the one who asserts the contrary opinion to received wisdom, and she does it in her version of English – much as Stacy Aumonier's 'mechanic with soul' does in his short story *Man of Letters*

In fact, though Byatt describes this as a Norfolk story, there is precious little in it to identify its location. Neither time nor place is specifically mentioned, and neither is described. The rural location is implied by 'the other end of the village', to which the nurse is hurrying in the opening line. Hodd's 'turnits' and his turnip cutter might give a Norfolk feel to the story...but there is a turnip cutter standing in a Cumbrian garden I work in, and it hasn't been imported for show (unlike, I suspect, the one that stands, spruced up in a visitor attraction at Gretna Green). The village name, of Dulditch is one imagined and used by Mary Mann for many stories (including 32 in a collection, *The Fields of Dulditch* .), but in this particular story, Norfolk is neither mentioned nor described. The focus is tight on the narrator and the half dozen people she speaks with: Hodd and the boy, the nurse, Mrs Hodd, and two children by the hearth – and, I suppose, as a seventh, the eponymous Little Brother.

Description, as a means of establishing place and time, and adding authenticity or even credibility to a story, is an area for discussion. How much of it should there be? Here there is almost none. Mrs Hodd's lying-in room is simply described as 'bare'. The downstairs room has a 'fire,' and later, a 'filthy hearth.' The dead baby's bier has perhaps the biggest collection of descriptive words of any single item in the story – 'rude', 'towel', 'frowsy pillow' and 'two chairs.' Mrs Hodd's bed is 'squalid' and 'big.' This is spare writing indeed. The outside world, apart from that opening 'village,' is represented by 'farm-yard' and 'turnip house,' where Hodd is to be found. There are no trees, fields, buildings, or weather. One thinks of Hemingway's advice to leave out everything that is not the story!

One curious phrase, used twice, encapsulates the whole of the rest of the world, or at least, the forces that control the local social environment: 'parson's folks' – who might send Mrs Hodd 'a drop o' soup,' or later, in relation to the children, 'see 'em clothed.' These are the same people, one supposes, reduced to 'folkes' in Mrs Hodd's last speech. Our attention is always tightly held on the story being told. We are not shown anything that would fill the movie maker's screen with background or horizon.

That there is so little, throws emphasis on what there is: the insistent description of Hodd and his boy, and the two children by the fire, all of whom, in addition to their red hair, are wearing or sitting on sacks. In fact, the appearance of the third sack, that of the two children at the fireside, draws a surprised comment from the narrator....'again a sack!' and is used adroitly to draw our eye, I think, from the 'battered doll' which follows it, squeezed in before we are told of Mrs Hodd's 'big squalid bed.'

There is, of course, no need for Mary Mann to specify Norfolk, or the 1890s. She is writing about her 'here and now', and our 'there and then,' which is a perfectly adequate, and appropriate location for her story.

Mary Mann was the wife of a Norfolk farmer, and wrote about her world. She was writing at around the same time as Arthur Morrison and a little before Coppard came to publication. *Little Brother* is a well constructed, powerfully direct, yet nevertheless subtle piece of polemic storytelling, and one that drives the reader to a contemplation of the issues it raises.

3 GEORGE MOORE
AND THE UNTILLED FIELD

George Moore (1852-1933) was writing in the decades before and after the turn of the nineteenth century. He was a grand old man of letters when James Joyce was up and coming on the block. A meeting with the two promised fireworks, but didn't deliver. Joyce is said to have been indulgent, and Moore to have been cautious.

The two Irishmen could have sent the sparks flying, as Moore claimed to have invented the stream of consciousness! There were other rifts between them, not least class. Joyce had seen his family slide down the middle class spectrum. Moore was an Irish landowner, who bled his estate dry to feed his writing habit. In Adrian Frazer's excellent biography (Yale, 2000) I got the sense that Moore, who is perhaps best known for his novel of 'lower life', *Esther Waters*, would not have appreciated the idea of a life as low as mine reading him, let alone thinking it had an opinion worth sharing! Like Joyce however, he renounced his Catholicism, and turned his back on Ireland, so there was something in common, even if obliquely. Like Joyce he had a European sensibility, and his move to London from Paris was more for its cosmopolitanism than its Englishness.

As writers too, they had more in common than you might expect, in that they were both experimenters. What is remarkable about Moore is that he rarely repeated himself in form or style, and this is especially true of his novels. He published five collections of short stories in his lifetime. A sixth, *In Minor Keys* (Eakin & Gerber (eds), Fourth Estate, 1985), was compiled from his uncollected works and contains fourteen stories. The title is from Moore's own suggestion for the title of a projected collection of short stories, and was used in a passage quoted in Eakin & Gerber's informative introduction to theirs:

> 'The mere act of concluding often serves to break the spell; the least violence, the faintest exaggeration is enough; we must drop into a minor key if we would increase the effect, only by a skilful use of anti-climax may we attain those perfect climaxes – sensation of inextinguishable grief, the calm of resignation, the mute yearning for what life has not for giving. In such pauses all great stories end.'
>
> (from Moore's introduction to Dostoevksy's 'Poor Folk'.)

That he is writing here about endings is a bonus, I think! My excitement in the idea of being a writer was sparked by reading *A Portrait of the Artist as A Young Man* while at school. Joyce was my literary hero; but as I have aged, so I have turned progressively towards George Moore as the embodiment of that ideal.

It was Moore who alerted me to the possibility of doing without speech marks or indents to signal new speakers (thus throwing the responsibility onto their voices). He reassured me of the propriety of plundering my own and the lives of those around me for the stuff of my fiction. He showed me how to recycle what I have already written into larger pieces, or to raid those larger stories for stand alone pieces. He encouraged me to tinker with and to re-invent my techniques, rather than to hone and perfect what might become a consistent and recognisable brand.

His reputation in some ways suffered from his diversity and diminished, except among academics, after his death. Perhaps it is time for a revival, among general readers, and among writers.

A good starting point, especially for those of us particularly interested in the short story, would be to look at his 1902 collection, *The Untilled Field*. Written in English, translated into what Moore calls 'Erse,' and then re-published in English, the tale of the development of the collection is told in an author's Preface, and a 1926 note in my Ebury, 1936 edition. This authorial introduction is particularly interesting for the fact that it gives Moore's reasons for writing the stories, and what he thought their purpose should be. Simply, this was to 'furnish(ing) the young Irish of the future with models.'

Of this endeavour Moore goes on to say that, when the translations into 'Erse' were not being promoted by the Gaelic League he was 'driven to the bitter extremity of collecting his manuscript for a

London publisher.' Published in English, the stories became available to a far larger and wider audience, one which would read them without making a judgment related to that earlier intention. In 1914, a 'revised' edition was published by Heinemann, and this year, it's worth noting, was that of the publication of Joyce's *Dubliners*. Perhaps for that reason alone it might be thought natural to compare the two collections, but there are other tales of life that Moore's stories might stand next to. A lifetime later, the stories of Claire Keegan – I have Faber's 2007 collection, *Walk The Blue Fields* – might be worth the comparison, as they, unlike Joyce's stories, are predominantly rural, rather than urban in setting.

Another feature of Moore's Preface to *The Untilled Field* is that it gives us an order of writing. For those studying authorial development this might be of more interest, and I was surprised to see that the stories are published in reverse order of their writing.

There are fifteen tales in all, and as I approached them the question that had formed in my mind – helpfully or otherwise I am still not sure – was that of just what the author was drawing attention to with his striking title.

When reading my own work, prose or poetry, I try to give as little introduction as possible – the title of the piece and my name only, and preferably just the title. The concern is that you shouldn't, and perhaps can't prejudice an audience to what they are about to hear.

There's something similar about prefaces and introductions to books, except that with these I'm conscious that I have been prejudiced by reading them, or at least have had my attention drawn to something that I wouldn't otherwise have picked up. In the case of *The Untilled*

Field it's the way the collection was put together. Moore tells us that he felt 'authorised,' by his discussions with other Irishmen over the issue of the Gaelic Revival, and he lists several of the stories that flowed from that. Then, he suggests, the subject matter itself sparked several more. This second batch forms the opening stories, in the order he gives, implicitly, of writing them. One story is not mentioned at all, and that sits between this second, and early group in the printed edition. Two stories, according to a publisher's note, were removed and two, further stories seem to have been added in 1914 and 1931 respectively.

This level of detail makes it hard to read the collection without an awareness of the potential development of the author's intentions and techniques as the stories unfold. In fact, so strong was this feeling that I began to question the wisdom of collections as opposed to anthologies.

The stories that Moore gives us first, that second flush of writing, evince what his Preface tells us he sought to do: 'to paint the portrait of my country.' There are eight of them, just over half the collection, and, with characters spilling over from one to the other, they give us a series of events involving the peasants – Moore's word – and the priests of a rural Parish. Several themes run through the group, notably that of the personal influence, amounting to control, exercised by the priests over a population that is presented as being submissive, superstitious, and subject to a curious passivity. This, and the religious reasoning behind it is made explicit in the first story: 'Our will is the most precious thing in us and that is why the best thing we can do is to give it up....'

Constant too, is the distant presence of America, an escape for some, a place of banishment or exile for others. In fact, the first story is entitled *The Exile* and it tells of two brothers and the woman that one of them will marry, driving the other to emigrate. Nicely paired with it is the second story, *Home Sickness*, given a title, the ambiguity of which will become apparent. Here, James Bryden returns to his childhood village to recuperate from illness. He has been living in America, working in a Bowery bar. In the story *The Wild Goose*, the penultimate of the collection, and perhaps the most important – if we choose to see the collection as an entity – a visiting American reprises, and develops some of the same themes. Bryden gets nostalgic, and looks for what has changed, and what hasn't. Rather than development and progress, he sees stagnation and decay. He also falls in love with, and drifts into the promise of marriage with a local girl. A letter from 'home' however, reminds him of his Bowery life, and he knows that, his health recovered, he must return.

> 'He hurried away, hoping he would come back. He tried to think that he liked the country he was leaving....'

> 'And when the tall skyscraper stuck up beyond the harbour he felt the thrill of home....'

The ambiguity of the title is not merely that of which country is his true home, and which he is sickening for, but that in Ireland he sees the sickness of what was once his home. At the end of the story, having married, raised children and grown old in America, all Bryden can remember is the hills of Ireland, and the eyes of the girl he did not marry there. The story contains one of the most powerful statements I have found anywhere in Moore, and certainly in this collection: 'There is an unchanging, silent life within every man that none knows but himself...' I wonder to what extent this is Moore's insight into himself, and also why it resonates so strongly with me!

The earlier story too revolves around a marriage, that of Catherine to one of the two Phelan boys. The ills of Bryden's Ireland are here too, but focus is on the family and how it operates, how it fits in with the expectations and limited choices that seem available to the boys.

'Well, Pether, is it the cassock or the belt you're after?'

One brother, being brighter and bookish, is sent to be a priest; the other, in love with Catherine but rejected by her, is more at home on the farm. Catherine, unable to marry the brother she wants, goes into a nunnery. Moore then switches it about. The priesthood does not suit the clever brother, and his return precipitates Catherine leaving the nunnery, and the farmer brother must flee to America.

These two stories lead on to a group that are similar, but which in style tend to lose narrative in favour of dialogue. Another feature of Moore's preface is the discussion about the language used by the Irish peasantry, and by people telling stories of them. Without being heavy handed he catches an accent, and this raises the question of how accents not our own, but that we have heard can be used in writing to convey individual, representative, or stereotypical characters.

'She does like to be meeting Pat in the evenings...'

'Sorra sign,'

Choice of words, the way they are spoken, and the order they are put in, all denote ways of speech that we think of as dialect or accent, and which might belong to an individual we wish to endow with a set of generally accepted characteristics, usually observed from the outside.

In the half dozen stories that follow there are whole pages that could pass almost as stage scripts, where the story is progressed by what the characters say to each other, and there are places where the reported speech that carries the narrative between the dialogue retains the idiomatic structures of the spoken language.

A few extra themes are introduced, though the others are not relinquished. The concept of 'public works,' paid for by the state, but undertaken purely to provide labouring jobs is raised in *A Letter to Rome* and *A Play-House in the Waste*. These resonated for me because the most socially useful job I ever did was to run Job Creation schemes under Jim Callaghan's government in the nineteen seventies, and I recognise the element of futility that was, and is so easy to satirize.

'..the futility of the road would satisfy English ministers.'

'while the people are earning their living on these roads, their fields will be lying idle, and there will be no crops next year.'

Throughout these stories the dominance of the priest, overbearing, cajoling, bullying, driven by anger, frustration and belief, plays against the passivity and superstition of the people. Even Father MacTurnan, described by Moore as 'gentler' and 'pathetic' in comparison to Father Maguire whom he calls 'harsh,' has, in *A Letter To Rome*, suggested the revocation of the edict on celibacy for reasons of Catholic supremacy, and not for personal ones.

Earlier priests have been much more explicitly controlling:

> 'You won't go home when I tell you to do so. We will see if I can't put you out of the door.'

> 'Sure, didn't the priest threaten to turn him into a rabbit.....'

> '....and he spoke like one who is not accustomed to being disobeyed.'

> 'I don't want anyone to leave this room.......Sit down.....'

And manipulative:

> 'Why don't you come to me and ask me to make up a marriage for you?'

This last to Kate Kavanagh, who does, under pressure, let him. But in the next story, having barred her husband from the bedroom on his wedding night, she departs alone, for America!

Moore isn't entirely one-sided. In conversations like those between Father John and Father Tom Maguire, he gives an alternative approach that the priest could take, but which the younger man will not.

> 'Pleasure,' said Father Tom, 'Drinking and dancing, hugging and kissing each other about the lanes.'

> 'You said dancing-now I can see no harm in it.'

> 'There's no harm in dancing, but it leads to harm.

With *Julia Cahill's Curse*, which is not mentioned in the preface, we get to the change point. Whether this belongs to the earlier or later group I cannot say, but it is certainly different to the stories that have preceded it. That change is not so much in the subject matter as in the approach, for Moore picks up the idea of the visitor, and uses a first person narrator who interrogates the driver of his 'car' and gets out of him the story of the eponymous curse. My guess is that this belongs to the earlier stories, because the same approach is used in the next story, *The Wedding Gown*.

I was reminded of M.R.James by this story, though it is a ghostly, rather than a ghost story. In it an old woman nurses protectively, over the years of an immensely long life, the dress that she wore on her wedding day. Rescued from extreme poverty by relatives in whose house she goes to live. The old woman may have saved the dress, but her mind is disturbed, and only the daughter of the family has a genuine relationship with her. When that daughter is prevented from going to a ball, by lack of a dress, the old woman allows her to borrow what she has so carefully guarded. At the ball and wearing the dress, the girl gets a sudden premonition that the old lady has died, and returns home to find her body.

What gives the story its ghostliness is not merely that premonition, but the events around it. The old woman seems to have recovered her wits, and her rationality as she lends the dress, and the girl, who has suffered a morbid fear of seeing a corpse, finds in her dead granny's face a reassuring image of herself. There is also a sequence in which the old lady, as she is dying, relives the joy of her long remembered wedding day.

> '....the bells are ringing,' she said, and went to the kitchen door; she opened it, and under the rays of the moon she stood lost in memories....'

It is an emotional story, and one that reminds us that Moore was an emotional writer – unmarried, but perhaps not unloved, and certainly a man aware of the potency of human love, and of the potency of the memory of it.

The last two stories, which the Preface and author's and publisher's notes suggest were bolted on to what had already been published in an earlier edition, are quite different from all that preceded them, different in form and content. Of *The Wild Goose*, Moore says [it]'allowed me to seek an outline that eluded me in the first version.' Whether this was included in the earlier collection I do not know, but he goes on to say that 'and should I find the needed outline, the story will become, perhaps, dearer to me than the twelve that precede it and that need no correction.'

The strong implication is that there was, in the collection, an earlier version, and that it was not the last of the stories – *The Fugitives* replaces two that were withdrawn in 1914, so there must have been sixteen at one time.

If the stories of what I have called the earlier stories are generally more diverse than the later eight, then *The Wild Goose* would not be a surprising find among them. It involves Ned Carmady – whose name we don't get until the fourth page – an American who visits Ireland, stays, falls in love, and marries. The marriage though, founders on the fact that he has been pushed into politics by his young lover, and his politics – anti-clerical – conflict with her Catholicism. Eventually he leaves. Ned is an American only by adoption, having moved to England as a child, and then to America via Europe as a young man.

The re-written version is newer than *Home Sickness*, but the original must have preceded it, which makes for an interesting speculation if that preface has tempted us into the comparison. *The Wild Goose* is longer, and fuller, and gives Carmady, towards the end, the opportunity for a philosophical explanation of his – or perhaps Moore's view of Ireland.

> 'Jesus himself was a heretic, St. Paul was another, and so was St.Patrick.'

And so was James Joyce, and George Moore was another.

Yet *Home Sickness* seems somehow more compact and compressed, and focussed, and has that powerfully resonant statement quoted earlier, bringing the story to bear more heavily on the individual, yet being about all men, whereas Carmady's story seems to be more universal – by virtue of his philosophical rant, yet ends being about a single man, who goes off to 'fight the stranger' in the Boer War. Stories often pass from the individual to the archetypal, but not necessarily in the same direction.

I began reading with the collection's title in mind, and I found it a few stories in, embedded, as the best titles often are, in a passing remark, as part of a larger statement. It turns up in that pivotal story,

Julia Cahill's Curse.

'And I noticed that though the land was good, there seemed to be few people on it, and what was more significant than the untilled fields were the ruins for they were not the cold ruins of twenty, or thirty, or forty years ago when the people were evicted and their tillage turned into pasture - the ruins I saw were the ruins of cabins that had been lately abandoned.....'

Her curse has been that each year a roof would fall in and a family go to America.

There is much in the lives of the people who populate these stories that is 'untilled.' References to waste, and futility, the decay of practices and misuse of resources occur throughout. Pether, in *The Exile* is, and will become no farmer, yet what he could become is not even given consideration. At the other end of the collection, in *The Wild Goose*, Carmady's political aspirations founder along with his marriage.

The last story, *Fugitives*, presumably written when the revised edition was issued, over twenty years after that first 'Erse' publication, is told in two parts. The first is set mostly in Dublin, where a sculptor finds a model to sit, nude, for his statue of the Virgin. She is sixteen, he twice her age. They do not become lovers, but he knows his statue will be his masterpiece. The priest who has commissioned the piece, though, has not expected a nude sitter to be used, and the statue, along with other pieces is destroyed.

The second half of the story is set in London, where Rodney, the sculptor plans a trip to Italy. He talks with two other exiles, one called Carmady. The other has met the statue's sitter, and has rescued her from an unwise, unfunded flight to London, returning her to her parents in Ireland. She is married off, to an American, who will take her home to an unfulfilled, circumscribed life.

It is difficult to interpret Moore's last story, added to the collection less than a decade before his own death, as other than being about him, and about the Artist-in-Exile – Joyce was in Paris, writing *Finnegan's Wake* at this time and Moore had spent most of his life as an exile, since his days among the Parisian artists.

The Untilled Field, perhaps because of its genesis and evolution is a broader read than the title, and the obvious themes suggest. It is wide in its understanding, but also in its approaches, and techniques. This breadth, of the writing style and in subject matter, is a hallmark of all Moore's work, and perhaps one of the reasons why his identity, and profile as a writer has been hard to brand, and to preserve.

At the end of the last story, Rodney recounts how two priests in Dublin discussed the ethical issue of the nude sitter, and gives us their conclusion:

> 'bad statues are more likely to excite devotional feelings than good ones, bad statues being further from perilous nature.'

It might be taken as Moore's summary of why the fields remain untilled.

4 BELISAIRE'S PRUSSIAN BY ALPHONSE DAUDET

Perhaps better known for his charming stories about Provence, first published in 1866 as *Lettres de Mon Moulin,* Alphonse Daudet (1840-1897) also wrote many stories set in Paris during the time of the siege in 1871. One of them was called '*Belisaire's Prussian*' and ends with the sentence 'It was my Prussian who was coming down on the current, in the middle of the stream.' This Prussian has been killed by Belisaire, and dragged across mudflats to be thrown into the River Seine.

The changes one might make to the ending of a short story need not involve re-writing. Merely moving the words around might be sufficient to have a discernible effect. That last sentence in *Belisaire's Prussian* is an 'open' sentence, by which I mean that its constituent parts add incrementally to what is already fully comprehensible, rather than compounding what does not yet make sense. Reverse the parts and you get: 'In the middle of the stream, coming down the current, was my Prussian.' This is a 'closed' sentence, where there is no meaning until the final piece is in place.

Either, as a sentence, makes sense in both French and in English, but the emphasis, in the closed version, would be thrown very strongly on 'my Prussian,' drawing attention to both the corpse, and to its connection with Belisaire, who is, apparently, telling the story. Even a change such as this, would have changed the focus of the story, and in a particular way. As published, in the English translation, the emphasis is on where the corpse is, not on who is responsible for it.

Were we to consider this last view of the story with 'my Prussian' in focus, we might be drawn to reflect upon what had happened in the story on the way to that conclusion. When this happens at the end of stories, I think of them as being 'reflective' stories. The most obvious example I know of is Hemingway's *'A Canary for One'*, where the last ten word sentence re-contextualises the entire preceding story, making what has seemed a random collection of disjointed observations into an entirely coherent set of responses by a narrator who is in a specific and hitherto undisclosed state of mind.

But *Belisaire's Prussian* leads us to consider that eponymous corpse 'in the middle of the stream,' centre stage, as it were, and as far away from that 'my' as it could be, and still be in the same sentence. The fact that the Prussian has featured in the title is significant. We have been looking for him, in a sense, all through the story, and may have thought that we had found him in the cellar where he was murdered. But it is only in the last sentence that the true echo of the title is heard, when Belisaire refers to him by that 'my. Daudet has to make sure that we know it is specifically 'Belisaire's Prussian' that the crowd is watching, and his ending demands that we consider him as he re-appears, as seen from the bridge at Villeneuve, told in the past tense, but frozen in the continuous present of the story's last words.

What if we took the entire sentence away, and ended the story one sentence earlier, what would we get? 'At a distance it had the appearance of a wherry.' To understand this, we have to have the preceding sentence: 'As I passed the bridge at Villeneuve the people were gazing at something black in the water.' Would either of them do the job of ending the story?

In fact, neither mentions a corpse, let alone one belonging to anybody. We would be left to guess what they were looking at, and with no certainty that we would guess rightly.

We could scrape away a little further, and end the story at the preceding paragraph. That describes Belisaire, telling of how 'a puff of wind' freed the Prussian's body from its 'moorings,' releasing it into the slow flowing Seine. It ends 'I took a draught of water, and quickly mounted the bank.'

This might be an ending for the story. We know what has happened, and to whom. The events have been completed, the body has been disposed of. But there is a curious lack of significance in it, though we would be predisposed perhaps, to review the events leading up to that moment – another reflective story, but hardly a revelation of something we didn't already know, nor a deepening of our understanding of what we did. Certainly not a prompt to imagination of what must surely follow. Daudet's tale, ended here, would simply fall apart, becoming a series of events, plausible enough, but without a point to their telling. Attributed to V.S.Pritchett is the assertion that a short story must 'reveal' what the real events would 'only suggest.'

Perhaps it's time to review those events. Belisaire's tale, which is told in the first person, has him crossing the Prussian lines at the end of the Siege of Paris to check upon a cottage he has abandoned. He takes with him his little son. The cottage has been trashed by the Prussians, and he encounters one – whom later we find out is called Hoffman – who draws his sword. Belisaire kills him, and taking his son with him flees back to the city. But then, fearing that if the body is found a neighbour left within the Prussian lines might suffer, he resolves to return and, at some risk to himself, to get rid of the body – hence the river, and all that we have seen.

There is, however, a complicating factor, for it is not actually Belisaire who is telling the tale, but another anonymous first person narrator. The tale begins, 'Here is a story that I heard this very week.' This narrator tells us something about the story too: that it was told in an accent foreign to his own, an accent that is tied not only to place, but to class, for Belisaire wears 'a great carpenter's apron.' We are told that the story was 'lugubrious and veracious' and that in Belisaire's voice it would have made our 'flesh creep' and 'blood run cold'; and that it was told to 'boon companions.' Our attitude towards Belisaire might be further influenced by one more authorial – or rather narrator's – intrusion, which is the parenthetical remark that Belisaire has said 'amnesty' when he meant 'armistice,' a curious slip, considering the content of his tale. This opening narrative is not the first part of a beginning and ending frame, for Daudet does not bring back his anonymous narrator at that ending. He uses him only to introduce the story, and to prejudice our hearing of it; or at least to give us some opinions upon it against which we might compare the telling we receive. If all stories, and especially the ones we call short stories, work by a progressive and incrementally increasing contextualisation of what follows, the beginning of a story is likely to kick-start that process in a fundamental way. Where we set out from is second in importance to where we are going. The relationship between the two, rather than, as in a novel, the journey itself, is the strength of the story.

The fact that Daudet has made Belisaire's narrative a story re-told by another narrator raises a number of questions. Is the significance of the story the same for Daudet's narrator and for Belisaire? Is it for us? Or for Daudet himself? What are we to think of the story, and the way it is told, and what do the tellers both, or even all three, think is the point of telling it, a point that must be what the ending will have focussed us on? What do we think it would have said on the tin? And what did we find in it? We could even speculate about whether or not Belisaire, when telling it originally, had ended where Daudet's narrator does.

Susan Lohafer, in an essay I often recall, about the 'storyness' of stories (in *The New Short Story Theories*, ed Prof.Charles E.May,Ohio,1994) talks of possible premature endings being found within short stories: places where they might have ended, but did not. Two such places – the suggested number – might be found in this story. One we have already dismissed – where Belisaire sees the body float free, and leaves the river bank. Another might be where he decides, having escaped successfully with his son from the scene of the killing, to venture to return and dispose of the body.

> 'There was no risk of our being fished out of the crowd. Then I only thought of our little cottage. The Prussians would surely burn it.... to say nothing of the risk to Jaquot, my neighbour.......
>
> I felt that I must arrange for the concealment of the body....'

Finished at this point, the story would leave us wondering about what happened next. Would he succeed? Would he get caught?

Such endings project us into the imagined future. Ambrose Bierce has several like this, *The Coup de Grace* being perhaps the most obvious. But Daudet too, has used at least once, this projective ending, in his story, *The Boy Spy*. Another siege story, this one sees a boy lured by greed and peer pressure into revealing to the Prussians plans that are being made to mount a raid across the lines. Knowing he has done wrong, he confesses all on his return to his father who in response takes a rifle and the coins his son has been paid and goes to join in the attack. Almost unnecessarily – to contemporary short story attuned eyes – we are told that he is never seen again.

Daudet's choice of ending for *Belisaire's Prussian* though, brings us to a consideration of the situation as is. It tells us of the re-appearing body, which we know is connected to Belisaire, and which is now, viewed by the Parisians, 'in the middle of the stream'. What are we to make of it? We must remember that Belisaire is telling this story, or rather, was overheard telling it. Is he proud of his actions? Did he step forward, as in a sense he does in the telling, to take the credit for them? Does Daudet or his narrator salute, or belittle him by the re-telling? The floating Hoffman is a stark image, and might be a potent symbol; but of what, and to whom? What does his presence there, killed, not in pursuance of his military objectives, but in a hand to hand fight with a civilian, what does it mean to us? The answer, I suspect, will vary from person to person, depending upon attitudes to war, to this war in particular, and to mortality in general. The story though, for each of us, whatever conclusions we finally draw, will have brought us to the point of having to interpret and evaluate its closing image.

> 'It was my Prussian who was coming down on the current, in the middle of the stream.'

5 HOW TO CURE A FUSSY WIFE BY JUSTUS VAN EFFEN

I'll confess, I'm partial to reading short stories from long ago. A story not worth reading ten years after it was written, probably wasn't worth reading anyway; possibly wasn't worth writing. But how about stories from a hundred years ago, a thousand even?

I've been working my way through Hammerton's nineteen thirties' twenty volume set, *The World's Thousand Best Stories* – of all times and all countries, allegedly. It's a real treasure trove for the short story addict, and for me, full of writers I've never heard of. Full too, of stories that spring into the imagination with all the freshness and vigour of the day that they were written. Some are unbelievably modern, and apart from technological references, could have been written yesterday, this morning even.

Occasionally though, that lapse of time and culture throws up a story that's hard to take; so far out of touch with the way we live and think now, that it can't be deemed acceptable, apparently. Such a one is *How To Cure A Fussy Wife*, by the Dutch writer Justus Van Effen (1684-1735). For the last five years of his life Justus ran the journal 'Hollandsche Spectator', modelled on the London Spectator, and this story is cast in the form of a letter written to that publication.

It tells of a visit to a friend's house, where, over a spotless table-cloth, a boorish husband rebukes his wife for an imagined rudeness to the visitor. The row escalates, with the husband spilling, first drops, then a glass, and finally, with deliberation in a sustained demonstration of husbandly superiority, a whole bottle of red wine – all over that beautiful white linen.

'...in pouring out, he allowed a drop every now and then to spill...'

'and when he considered he had spilt enough sufficient wine everywhere...'

He then gives the wife a lecture on her place, his authority, and the option of taking it, or leaving him! At which point the eponymous lady caves in, offers suspiciously over-the-top apologies both to her husband and to their guest, and confesses her undying love, and the two perform a tearful re-union.

Out-shrewing the tame ending of Shakespeare's play – which modern directors still struggle to make acceptable to us –the bent of Justus' story seems wholly indefensible. It is nothing more than an exhibition of naked male superiority: a misogynist tract:

> 'Be absolutely assured that I wish to be and shall be master in my house.'

But, if we recall the very beginning of the story, another perspective emerges. The first person narrator, and writer of the letter, tells how, pre-occupied with his thoughts, he has entered his friend's house without wiping his feet at the door. He is more than embarrassed by the trail of footprints he leaves upon the marble floor, and hastens back to the mat to clean his shoes. He was 'displeased with myself'. The lady of the house is displeased too, and, 'after some considerable grumbling' orders the maid to clean up the mess. Nevertheless, she greets her visitor 'with politeness' and conducts him to the dining room. It is the narrator's comment though, as he berates himself for his fault, which we should notice.

> 'I have always considered it to be an incivility, and even a thing contrary to good-nature, to spoil the work of others, especially since it requires so little trouble on one's part to avoid the same.'

The dining room is 'the pink of neatness', and it is here that the events previously sketched out take place. It is a short, short story, occupying just over four printed pages. The events themselves are completed, at the beginning of the last paragraph, with the comment: 'This determined the happily ended tragedy.' But the paragraph goes on - and here we must remind ourselves that it is in the form of a letter for publication - pointing out that on many subsequent visits the narrator has witnessed the wife behave with 'respectful submissiveness.' His final sentence, though, nails who is being satirized by the events described:

> 'It was she herself who urged me, Mr Spectator, to inform you of this incident'

And note the way the author has him remind us of the public nature of the story. The wife's reasons for this, he tells us, are 'to cause repentance in masterful and foolish women,' which looks to me like undiluted irony.

It's sometimes easy to overlook the fact that the subject of a satire can be presented as if they were the hero of the story. It's the literary equivalent of giving somebody enough rope, and watching as they hang themselves.

The story is told is a very straightforward way, as if it were indeed a letter to a journal recounting an actual event. There seems no real dialogue, although the husband and wife both get almost a page of speech each, as they put forward their cases. The wife too has several pieces of direct speech attributed to her. Perhaps it's the layout on the page that deceives, for the lightness of verbal exchange that we are used to, where alternate speakers barely fill their single line, is missing here. The four and a quarter pages of text are in solid blocks, with only fifteen paragraphs in the whole, and several of them quite short. Half of the story is in the two great chunks of the husband's assertion of, and the wife's submission to his unreasonableness! We overlook, perhaps, the fact that realistically, one could not reconstruct, word for word, the length of speeches here given, from the recollection of such a visit.

A curiosity of the telling, to modern eyes, is that the writer slips, seemingly at random, from the past to the present tense, as he tells his tale. Writing of the wife's developing reaction to her husband's tirade....

> 'they [her eyes] gradually filled with tears, no longer of rage, but of remorse and love. Without a word she throws her arms around his neck,...'

Sometimes he moves the other way:

> 'After this, having once more embraced her husband, she runs out of the room,...'

Followed, a line or two later by:

> 'During dessert they fell into a new dispute....'

It is the attitude of the narrator, or letter writer, that directs our response. He does not call his friend a fool, but calmly reveals him to be one.

Anyone who has followed my blog will know that from time to time I indulge in the harmless pleasure of re-writing stories from long ago, and seeing how they look dressed in contemporary clothes – *Henry & Mr Ouffle*, recently read at Liars League's Hong Kong enclave was such a one…the original *Mr Ouffle* having been written by the seventeenth century L'Abbe Bourdelot.

I wonder how Van Effen's story would fare under such a transformation?

6 FELLOW TRAVELLERS: PRITCHETT, BATES & MANSFIELD

Three short stories I've read over the past few years caught my attention for a very particular reason. They are *The Station*, by H.E.Bates, *Many Are Disappointed*, by V.S.Pritchett, and *The Woman at the Store*, by Katherine Mansfield. What I couldn'rt decide was whether they were the same story in three guises, or three different stories in the same vein.

What links them is the situation in which their various characters are placed, despite those places being widely dissimilar. In fact, it is not only the situations, but the structure of the stories that draws attention to the similarities between them. All three involve a party of travellers arriving at an isolated location, where a woman offers hospitality. In Bates' story she is alone, in the other two, accompanied by a child. In all three she is a married woman whose husband is not present. In Mansfield's story, the husband may have been murdered. In all three cases the travellers are a party of men (although in Mansfield's story, a woman in the group narrates the story).

The openings are similar in function, but are handled differently. Bates' might be regarded as the most straightforward:

> 'For thirty seconds after the lorry had halted between the shack and the petrol pumps the summer night was absolutely silent'

The locating of stories in time and place seems to me always to be a prime function of their beginnings. It gives mood, context, often implies themes, and introduces characters, and can be either deepened or subverted as the story continues. In *The Station* there's an extra resonance for me, for I not only grew up at a petrol station, but I worked the twelve hour weekend night shifts at a motorway service station when I was a student. It was a real life location that called travellers from the darkness, and sent them off into it again after our encounters.

Mansfield's story is not set in darkness, but it is located as precisely as Bates'.

'All that day the heat was terrible.'

Both these authors go on to fill out the descriptions. Mansfield reveals the narrative voice in her long second sentence, when 'white pumice dust swirled in *our* faces,' (italic, mine). Bates introduces 'the driver and his mate' eight lines in, at the beginning of his fourth sentence.

Pritchett's opening contrasts by its brevity, but fulfils the same functions:

> 'Heads down to the wind from the hidden sea, the four men were cycling up a deserted road in the country.'

He goes on, of course, to fill out his description too, but it's not the weather or terrain I want to point out next. It's the first mention of the woman.

> '...he whispered out of one corner. 'See her? She heard us come.'

> '...and there's a girl at the pub, a dark girl with bare arms and bare legs in a white frock.'

> '...'Don't forget there's a woman too, Jo, with blue eyes and yellow hair, who'll promise you something else before she shakes hands with you.''

If you must know, Bates, Pritchett, and Mansfield was the order, but it's the similarities that interest. Each, in its way links promise, or at least expectation – though not the same one – with the woman, and both of those qualities make a good opening for a short story.

Mansfield has made us wait more than a page, for her woman, whereas Bates has given us half a page. Pritchett, though, has sprung his on us within three lines. Differences and similarities, when found together, are always instructive. What these three writers do before they give us their lone women, is to contextualise them. Bates gives his woman the darkness and isolation of the night service 'shack,' and we see her in it through the eyes of Bates' two travellers. Mansfield gives us the journey to the remote 'store,' and something of the attitude of the character the narrator will concentrate on. He sings a song, of which we are given enough to make something, even if we do not know the rest.

> 'I don't care, for don't you see,
> My wife's mother was in front of me!'

Pritchett too, has given us context and expectations with those 'heads down,' and his description of the girl. Also, all these words are taken in light of the titles, which themselves contextualise the whole story.

Look at those titles. A 'station' is not a random place. It is an official stopping point on a journey, a place where destinations are implied. It also has the smack of authority. People are 'stationed,' as perhaps the woman, whom it has been implied is listening out for arrivals, has been. The travellers on are more than a simple journey by road.

Mansfield's title draws our attention to her woman, which

makes the delay in her appearance a period of anticipation rather than of ignorance. Pritchett's title suggests, because of the proximity to it of that 'girl' perhaps, that it is the woman in whom we shall be disappointed. Yet when the title is echoed, early on in the story, it is spoken by the woman, and relates to the fact that her house, though known as 'the tavern', is not in fact a pub, and serves only 'teas.' All the men, she implies, will be disappointed, and the story might tell us how.

The characters in these diverse stories share similarities and differences. Bates has the simplest group: the driver and his mate: an older, and a younger man. Mansfield adds a third, and her narrator, as has been mentioned, is a woman. One of the other two, the man with the song, is her brother, and the other, possibly her partner, though it is not made clear. In fact, the character Jim seems mainly to provide someone for the narrator to converse with, and by whom Jo will be given information that the author does not want to put into the narrator's mouth. In Pritchett's story the four cyclists are subtly differentiated. A feature common to all the stories is that the travellers observe each other, and in Pritchett's story, which has the largest number of them, it is the most significant element, at least in terms of the amount of story taken up with it.

The more characters there are in the group, perhaps inevitably, the more they have to be differentiated, and the more they can be, allowing the story to develop facets of perception and insight. Pritchett's story has five to play with, six including the woman's child. The adults each have their own interests, and descriptions:

> 'Bert, who was the youngest...'

> '...Sid on his pink racing tyres, who was the first to see it, the first to see everything.'

> 'Harry's ruddy Roman road'

> 'Ted, the oldest and the married one..'

> 'She was a frail, drab woman, not much past thirty...'

Curiously, Bates' woman too 'seemed about thirty.' Mansfield's woman is harder to see.

> '...a woman came out, followed by a child and a sheep dog – the woman carrying what appeared to me a black stick.'

The descriptions of her become more unflattering, - 'ugly,' 'figure of fun,' 'sticks and wires,' 'front teeth knocked out,' - but she is alone, and vulnerable, and so in his way is Jo, who Jim reminds 'at any rate, my buck, she's female flesh.' That potency of 'female flesh' is present and powerful in all these stories, however it is presented.

If the stories had only one traveller, the encounters, and the way we perceive them would be quite different. Whatever narrative voice was used, it would be only one voice. In all these stories it is the different viewpoints, in relation to the woman, and to the other characters, that enables the author to get us to a point where we have to form our own view.

This view will be primarily of the one character in particular whose relationship to the woman is singled out. This character gets an offer the others, other in the case of the driver, cannot even fully comprehend, and which they don't necessarily even recognise as having been made.

In Bates' story, the woman waits 'in an attitude of unsurprised expectancy,' before she offers them both food. The driver orders his usual, but the mate – whom the woman has not seen before and who is already transfixed 'in admiration' - is offered something different 'with a kind of soft and indirect invitation.' The offer of fruit is also made, which causes the driver, innocent of the innuendo that we will pick up, to enthuse about the 'plums' that the woman can provide. After the meal proper, she leads the two men out into the darkness with a torch – the lorry driver has ventured on his own, but found only green plums by the light of failing matches. As she shines the torch for him to stuff his face with ripe fruit, she helps Albie, the mate, to fill his pockets in the darkness, all the while 'keeping her other hand still on his, pressing it against her by an almost mechanical process of caressing.'

It is a powerful seduction, and masterly in that the innuendo of 'plums,' so commonplace to British humour, does not spoil the scene by triggering our laughter. The driver's continued enthusiasm, for the plums purely as fruit, contrasts with our recognition of what the mate appears to have been offered, and to have responded to. Yet nothing has been made explicit.

Mansfield's woman is more direct, and indeed her story is more explicit. She has the reputation of knowing 'one hundred and twenty five ways of kissing,' though Jo is not told of this, but she offers him a room of his own, and in the night the other two hear 'the sound of a door being opened – then shut to.'

In Pritchett's story, there is neither the sensuality of Bates' tale, nor the explicitness of Mansfield's, but there is a close exchange between the woman and one of the cyclists. Sid's 'trouble' we are told is that he has 'seen too many girls before,' and it is he who goes to pay the woman at the non-alcoholic tavern, after they have taken her afternoon tea. He is the only one to speak to her alone, and their conversation, though subtly so, is knowing. They understand each other, in a way that the others could not understand either of them.

> '.....she saw the deep serious shadows of his eyes and the pale drooping of the naked lids. The eyes looked tired

and as if they had seen many things and she was tired too.'

Though it is slight, Pritchett's drawing of our attention to that mutual tiredness brings these two characters closer together than any other two in the entire tale. The narrator has described Sid, and the woman more fully elsewhere, but never with the depth of empathy implied by this couple of lines.

These three special encounters occur towards the end of their respective stories. Then we are left with endings that must act as some sort of window on what we have witnessed. In Pritchett's case, in keeping with the tone of the story, it is a subtle focus, on the ring that Sid wears as the four cyclists pedal off, in search of a proper pub. This ring, the others said of 'Move that up a couple and he'd be spliced,' but Sid says, to the woman's child 'Keep a ring on your little finger and you'll be lucky.' And of the woman, he says 'She's got hers on the wrong finger.'

The endings of the other two stories also see the travellers leaving, though in Mansfield's story Jo is left behind to an uncertain fate, and Bates' driver and his mate will return. As they drive off the younger man eats a plum, and is 'trembling.' The very last images though, of these two stories, are almost interchangeable:

'And glancing back again he could see nothing of the station but the red sign flashing everlastingly out and on, scarlet to darkness, *The Station* to nothing at all.'

'A bend in the road and the whole place disappeared.'

Intentionally perhaps, these two disappearances give a mythical quality to the locations, and Bates' for me, especially so.

A question remains though, which is to what extent the witnessing of those special encounters, within the broader meetings, is the true focus of each of these stories. Could it be that, as the party of visitors gets bigger, the focus is progressively shifted away from that, and towards the differences between the visitors themselves?

You might ask what use it is to make such a comparison between three such stories, with their similarities and differences, which after all, are probably co-incidental. It could be that they offer us the sense of a story framework that despite the similarities still allows of quite different stories to be told. For a reader that is surely interesting, for we are being manipulated by stories in our perceptions of ourselves, and of the life around us. As writers, it might be useful, when we are attempting the manipulations.

7 NEXT TO GODLINESS
BY MATT PLASS

I know nothing about Matt Plass, other than what it tells me, which is precious little, in the anthology in which I found his story. It's the Fiction Desk anthology 'New Ghost Stories II,' and *Next To Godliness*, it says, is Matt's fourth appearance with Fiction Desk.

None of this matters of course, except perhaps, to him.

I can remember, when at school in the sixties, asking an English teacher why we didn't study such writers as Alistair Maclean, who was currently popular. His answer was that we didn't yet know how good they were. I've pondered that reply over the years, because I do find it particularly challenging to assess contemporary writing.

Matt Plass's *Next to Godliness* is a clever little story, but despite its position in the New Ghost Stories II anthology, by

Fiction Desk, it isn't really a ghost story. It is a good story, perhaps even a haunting one.

It's one of those stories where the past, the back-story of the characters, is revealed bit by bit, and with that revelation comes a deeper understanding of their present, and from that understanding springs our ability to feel the significance of what we are being told at the end

There are only three types of short story, classified by their endings. There is the type, like Hemingway's *A Canary For One*, that makes us look back over the journey we have taken through the story, and re-evaluate it. There is the type that, like *A Telephone Call*, by Dorothy Parker leave us exactly where we started, but with a changed perception of precisely where that is. And there is the type like *Next To Godliness*, in which we are confronted with a future for the story that we cannot help but imagine.

The launch pad that will project us into this future is carefully constructed, in the conversations of the protagonists, a married couple whose relationship is under strain from a past catastrophe that we soon guess at. But strange things are happening in their house, things that each must blame upon the other, for each knows that he, and she, is not responsible for them. When one of the partners discovers the truth, it is shocking to them, but the realisation, by both the character in question, and the reader, is that it will be far more shocking for the other. More importantly, it will be the partner who has found the truth that will have to bring it to the knowledge of the other, and perhaps we question whether either of them, let alone the relationship, will survive the revelation.

The unease, is introduced early and very subtly in the husband's first person narrative: 'Mary's washed the dishes; a concession, perhaps.' Then, 'I've also *gotta rush*' seems slightly grudging. But at the end of the same paragraph, the tension is explicit: 'To do otherwise would be a declaration of war.'

One element that contributes to the tension we feel here, is that it's hard, impossible even, to decide who we should side with. Both protagonists seem at times, to be in the wrong. When the husband chalks on the chalkboard, *'forgot you tidied my book?'* we wonder if he is making too much of it. When he goes to the pub alone, and meets his friends there, we know by their greeting that something has been going on for some time: 'How are you bearing up?'

The strangeness of what lies between this couple is brought home when he finds the usually untidy cupboard has been more than merely tidied: 'Every jar and packet is aligned.'

We soon learn that somebody has to be not telling the truth, unless something very strange indeed is happening – which is where the ghost story element comes in.

> ''You think that it was me who rearranged the kitchen,' I say.'

It is a first person narrative, but we do not immediately trust the narrator nor assume it to be a tale told by the more favoured character. Many a tale has been narrated by the villain!

A crisis point is reached, and the final element of back-story revealed, when the shrine-like room of their deceased daughter is tidied. He mistakes this for a 'good' sign of Mary's recovery. She accuses him of sacrilege. When both are convinced that the other is telling the truth, she comes to believe that the dead Alicia has returned to put the house right.

'She's trying to help.'

The revelation revitalises Mary 'Aren't you excited?' but he is devastated by this change in her.

''Oh, no'

No, no, no, no.''

And for a while perhaps, we are seduced into imagining a ghostly explanation for what is going on. The desperation of both parties, to deal with what afflicts, and affects them both, is mirrored by our concern to understand and to judge between them, or perhaps our struggle to accept the ghostly explanation that is on offer.

If truth is stranger than fiction, then here, in this fiction, the fact is stranger than the supernatural alternative. Yet it is clever, elegant even, and, in the end, not without precedents almost as strange in the real world. But the fantasy that has been constructed by one of the protagonists has brought with it a sort of relief from the pain of that back-story, and when the truth comes out, as the other partner must make sure it does, that pain must surely flood back in again.

Driven to the certainty that his wife's behaviour is not only irrational, but perhaps unconscious, for she denies it, the husband lies in wait for her with his camera.

> 'In the end I sit on the toilet with the lid down, the bathroom door open a fraction of an inch, ready to capture Mary when she reaches the top stair. I need proof; for her, not for me.'

But it is not Mary he captures.

> 'these are light steps. Lighter even than Mary's dancer's tread, light enough to belong to a child?'

This is the most ghostly point in the story, where no other explanation seems possible. For a moment he too believes that it is their dead daughter who has returned. But, of course, it is not. It is Georgie, 'a woman in her fifties.' Driven by her own demons, she breaks into other people's houses, and cleans them. With her testimony, and the film he has shot, the narrator not only can, but must disillusion his wife of her belief in the ghostly child.

Among much that I like about this story, is the fact that

such a wildly unlikely explanation seems, in its context, so perfectly fitting. The power of the story though, is packed, as in all the best stories, within that last line:

'Then, with Georgie's help, I will take from Mary, for the second time, the one thing no-one can afford to lose.'

8 THE BLUSH
BY ELIZABETH TAYLOR

What made me choose this short story to write about was the sense of shock I experienced when I reached the end. Two things contributed to that shock. The first was that I had forgotten the title of the story, of which the ending, as you will see, reminded me. The other was the fact of the ending itself, not so much an extension of the events in the story, but a reaction to them.

For the end of *The Blush* is that eponymous flush itself. It overtakes and engulfs the main protagonist of the story, as she considers the significance of what she has just been told by a third character in relation to what she has understood of the second character, who has been present in the earlier part of the story. I can't, at present, think of any other short story of the two or three thousand I have read over the last few years, that has given me an ending quite like this one.

Short stories are about their endings, of course, but this is the sort of short story that reminds you of that!

If one thinks about writing a blush into a story, something like 'she – or he – blushed' would suffice. But Elizabeth Taylor does not settle for that. 'Then she felt herself beginning to blush.' is the second sentence of the closing paragraph, and the following three lines develop that blush until even the character herself has to go 'over to a looking glass' and study 'with great interest this strange phenomenon.'

And it's one of those stories, that when you get to the end, sends you right back to the beginning, to think more deeply and again, about just what has caused that phenomenon.

There are two women in this story, 'Mrs Allen and the woman who came every day to do the housework.' It is about Mrs Allen – who will go on to blush for us. She has dreamed her life away into middle age. Childless, though she has dreamed of having children – 'their bibs at meal times,' 'the day the eldest boy would go off to boarding-school,' 'the pride of grief,' Mrs Allen has her regrets.

The precision of the detail is not only of how she lives, but how she dreams, and as her longings turn to sadness – 'I shall never have children now,' she tells herself - the life of Mrs Lacey, the cleaning lady, draws her to comparisons.

Mrs Lacey has a lot to complain of. Her boy is lazy, one daughter 'full of dainty ways,' the other 'moped and glowered and answered back.' They offer no help, earn no money; and Mrs Lacey 'envied her own daughters their youth.' Mrs Allen considers that her children would have been different, but she knows also that Mrs Lacey's might have been, for she has heard the gossip in the village.

Mrs Lacey goes to the pub, on her own. The children hang about outside. They are not well fed, or cared for. Mrs Lacey, for her part, envies the relative wealth of the Allens. They drink – a sherry on Sunday mornings – in the posher of the two village pubs, where people 'stood and sipped and chatted as at a cocktail-party'. Mrs Allen, however, thinks wistfully of the 'Horse and Jockey' where people 'sat down and drank, at tables all round the wall.'

Mrs Allen considers her own marriage: loveless as well as childless, with Humphrey 'earning more and more money.' Little is said of Humphrey, but in an image that may well echo later, we are told that Mrs Allen has spent 'a large part of her married life'.... 'listening for her husband's car,' including, perhaps significantly 'the door being slammed.'

The slow crisis of the story unfolds. Mrs Lacey falls pregnant, again, and not happily. She takes time off work. Mrs Allen does her own housework, resenting being let down. And then Mr Lacey arrives at the door, angry, and resentful too.

'It's too much for her.' He complains. The story comes out. He believes that, in addition to the daytime cleaning, his wife has been baby-sitting till late, for the Allens, while they go to cocktail parties. He is 'bewilderdly at sea'. 'Night after night', he complains. 'Let them stay home and mind their own children once in a while.'

He had been expecting a younger woman though, a 'flighty' one, but recognises 'something of himself in her, a yearning disappointment.' Mrs Allen too is surprised, for Mrs Lacey has said her husband is 'twenty years older than me.' This man 'looked quite ageless, a crooked, bow-legged little man.'

Mrs Allen promises not 'to ask her' anymore. His angers fizzles out and he leaves. She closes the door and listens to him 'wheeling his bicycle across the grass.' And then she blushes, and what makes this story so great is that we are not sure of what she blushing about, because there are so many elements here that could make her blush.

She has realised that Mrs Lacey's life is not what she thought it was, nor her husband the man she would have expected. Perhaps she has realised something about her own life. Perhaps she is blushing because she has not disabused Mr Lacey of his illusions, about her, about his wife, about Humphrey. Perhaps even, she might be blushing because she realises Humphrey is actually the one who brought Mrs Lacey home when Mr Lacey 'heard the car stop down the road'. The causes of the blush are as deep and as spreading as the blush itself, and our awareness of them spreads as widely as we re-consider, and re-read what we have read. Perhaps she is blushing at her own gullibility and lack of awareness. Perhaps she is blushing because 'She knew that it was a wasteful way of spending her years.'

Good story. Good writing.

9 SOMERSET MAUGHAM ADAPTED

Regular readers of my wordpress blog 'Bhdandme's blog' will know that I'm interested in text to film adaptations. A few nights ago I watched a couple of c1950 Gainsborough Films adaptations of Somerset Maugham short stories. *The Facts of Life* and *The Colonel's Lady* form half of a four part film called, inspiringly, *Quartet*.

An unexpected delight was to see Maugham himself, lizard-headed and oily, gold teeth glinting in the black and white footage, telling us about his life and his writing. There's something incredibly smug to the modern eye, at least to this one, about Maugham and his characters.

This is particularly true of the protagonists in *The Facts of Life*, where a middle class Nicky encounters a high-class tart in Monte Carlo. She's twenty, he's nineteen, but they both look middle aged, he in his gents' formal attire, she in her evening gown! The voices too are redolent of the upper class of a bygone era.

It's a good story. Nicky's father beefs to his fellow club members how his son has gone to Monte Carlo, for the first time unaccompanied, carrying with him the fatherly advice to not gamble, not to lend money, and to not get involved with women. Nicky of course gambles, and wins twenty thousand francs (100,000 in the film), lends a thousand (10,000 in the film), to a woman, whom he goes on to dine, dance, and have sex with (in the text)!

She, while he seems to sleep, raids his wallet and hides the money. He, having watched through half open eyes, returns the compliment, and retrieves it. In the morning they part, and he subsequently discovers he has taken not only his money, but the rest of her stash too.

On his return he rubs his father's nose in the bad advice. What should he do, the father asks his chums? Not to worry, old boy, they tell him, and the story (in the text) ends with the pithy comment that the boy is lucky, which is better than being 'born clever or rich' (which may well be true!).

What has always interested me in adaptations is the changes that are made to, or should that be from, the originals. Some of these can be put down to technological or financial limitations, but there are nearly always changes that cannot be explained away thus. They are the changes that are made for other reasons: changes where the story is being put to other uses, where it is being made to serve new agendas. These changes often reveal the motives, and natures of the film-makers, in stark contrast to those of the original writer (see *Blade Runner* for a classic example of this – Phillip K Dick thinking his replicants lesser beings for their lack of emotional sympathy, Ridley Scott – the film's director – thinking them superior). They also reveal something about the attitude of the film-maker towards the audience, and perhaps also imply something about that audience. Such is the case here, I think, for Maugham's audience as a writer, might have been, and probably was, significantly different, and was seen differently too, from that of 'the movies'.

I've mentioned already the changes to the amounts of money won and lent. What was that all about? Because curiously, whereas in the film those 100,000 francs are said to be worth one hundred pounds, in the book the twenty thousand franks are worth 'two hundred pounds roughly'. The book's exchange rate rings truer to me than the film's, and the story was collected in 1951, making it not far off contemporary with the film, though, presumably it could have been written several years earlier. Strange, I feel, that the film-maker should exaggerate the francs by such a multiplier, yet halve the English value attributed to them. What does that tell us about the target audience, and their sense of money?

One other change grabbed my attention: it was that in the film, Nicky does not sleep with the woman, and therefore is not told, as he leaves in the morning, that he is 'a sweet boy and a wonderful lover'. In the film Nicky sleeps on the couch, though he has been asked, before the lady retires to her bed, if there is 'anything' else that he wants! When she comes out in the night to steal his money we get an eyeful of her in her nightdress, but it is, I thought, a little less revealing than her evening dress was. Why so coy Gainsborough Films, when Maugham himself need not be? The answer must surely lie in what sort of audience the film was aimed at, and what sort of readership the book was intended for. Many of Maugham's stories – though by no means all – were set in the 'higher' echelons of society where attitudes to money, and morality, were quite different to those in the penny seats.

The second film, *The Colonel's Lady* was set in a similar class, but with an older generation. The eponymous heroine, a dowdy, middle aged woman, married to a boring and rather comic old buffer, has written without his knowledge a poetry book. Amazingly it becomes the talk of the town, and the club! She, rather than he, gets invited to dine with the local aristocracy on the back of it. He is bewildered, the more so, when his mistress and associates rave about the collection, which turns out to chronicle a steamy romance with a younger man who has died, leaving only the bittersweet memories.

The colonel is hurt, outraged too, believing that his dowdy wife must have had an affair. At the end his solicitor, who, like everyone else, has read the poems, advises him to let it go, to do nothing, and the colonel after huffing and puffing, agrees that's the best way. As with all good short stories the last few words are critical. 'The truth is, I don't know what I'd do without Evie' are not the last words, but they are Maugham's last manouvering of us into position to understand the statement that follows: 'But I'll tell you what, there's one thing I shall never understand till my dying day: What in the name of heaven did the fellow ever see in her?'

You might carp that I have referred to this closing sentence as a statement, when it clearly ends with a question mark. But the question asked by the colonel is the statement that Maugham is making at the end of his story. Our response as readers is not to answer it, but to reflect upon what it reveals about the colonel and his marriage, and by extension what it gives pause to thought for in our own relationships and those we witness around us.

So, it's a tragi-comedy. We know what the fellow saw, and we know what the colonel might have seen, and experienced, had he had the wit and sensitivity. Gainsborough Films though, don't have Maugham's degree of faith in us. They bolt on a schmaltzy ending.

It bolts on quite well. In fact, it fits in perhaps, with what we would wish for, with the 'pity' we might feel – to get a mite Aristotelian for a moment – for the colonel's, and the lady's predicament. But savouring that bittersweet taste of what might have been, had things gone differently, is not what Gainsborough think that their cinema-goers want.

In the film, there is a further scene, in which, and maybe you could guess it, the lady explains, when the colonel demands to know who the bounder was, that it is his younger self, and the days of their first love that she has written about. The film ends with his head pressed into her bosom, and I reach for a tissue! (seriously, I'm a sucker for a happy ending).

A friend of mine, and one of the best short story writers I have come across – unpublished in the main (what's wrong with you people?) - recently had a similar brush with a performance reading in the 'States, where the actor could not bring himself to deliver the lines of the downbeat ending of a short story, but demanded a Gainsborough-style re-write. If it wasn't potentially defamatory I'd share my friend's rant about this, it was so entertaining! A lifetime on from Maugham, some things haven't changed. Hollywood and its pale shadows still opt for escapism over reality.

An interesting speculation is as to whether or not Maugham approved of the addition. Clues in the text certainly suggest he would not have welcomed it: 'Damn it all, even ten years ago Evie was no chicken and God knows, she wasn't much to look at.' The negatives are deep rooted in the colonel, and even his lawyer can remark, 'after all, you're not in love with her, are you?' There's no hint really, that I could see in the text, that the colonel has merely forgotten, or grown out of a previous love. Yet, I suspect Maugham must have agreed to the addition. He was well enough known to have some say, and does introduce the stories in person. Perhaps they made him an offer he couldn't refuse.

And they have not necessarily damaged the story. What they have done though, especially by changing its ending, is to radically change its message. Films are so like short stories, in the importance invested in their endings. When the curtain closes and we leave the cinema, it is the endings, I suspect, which haunt us, just as the closing paragraphs, sentences, or even words, are what we dwell upon at the end of a short story. Change the ending, or change its significance by altering our route to it, and whatever else is left as in the original, the fundamental element of the story has been changed: it's purpose.

A story is not a sequence of events. It is a sequence of events related in such a way as to precipitate an emotional or intellectual reaction in its perceiver. Gainsborough Films, by that single extra scene, has turned Somerset Maugham's story completely around, has stood it on its head, and the reason for doing so was, I'm sure, to serve a target audience that the original text was not seeking to serve.

Quartet is available on dvd as part of a three disc set, with *Encore*, and *Trio*. I got my copy from Movie Mail, which you can find online. *The Collected Short Stories of Somerset Maugham* is in four paperback volumes from Penguin, now, I believe, available only second hand.

10 THE HEART OF THE WOOD
BY MRS W.K.CLIFFORD

Mrs Clifford's story, of a divorced woman who elopes with her lover, ends in tragedy, but one wonders if the tragic element is the same for us, as it was for the readers of her own time. The doomed affair ends in the eponymous wood, where the fleeing couple have bought a run-down country house. After a wonderful couple of years the woman is cut – we would say snubbed - while on a visit abroad, and this brings home to her the shame of her position. She goes into a terminal decline, and her bereaved partner lives out his life in the rambling house, surrounded by tramps and ne'er do wells whom he has taken in.

A theatrical man, he bolsters his failing spirits with theatrical flourishes, but when he dies, is buried alongside his lover in an unmarked grave, 'in the heart of the wood.' His will directs that the house itself is to be demolished, the wood sealed off for ten years, and then donated to the local community – and to passing tramps and gypsies.

This act of total self-effacement is reminiscent of Hardy's Mayor of Casterbridge – a novel that could aspire to short story status, almost! – but whereas Michael Henchard's has the whiff of petulant narcissism, Ackersley, the actor's, seems genuinely tragic.

It is a story of class, and of social expectations, and it is told in a straightforward way. In fact, it was the form rather than the content that made me add this story to my list of stories to write about.

'It was all the mother's fault:' the story begins. The mother, with dire warnings about actors, tries to put her daughter off, but the relationship continues. So, feigning illness, she takes the unfortunate Nina abroad and marries her off to a Marquis. The dumped actor despairs, and flees the country to make his fortune, but when he returns, and takes up again with London society, he seeks his former lover out. Divorce, and a Registry Office marriage follow.

The structure of the story is interesting, and in comparison to many others from the same period – Mrs Clifford, also known as Lucy Lane Clifford, was publishing from the mid 1880s to her death in 1929 – it is quite short at eight pages in the Hammerton *'World's Thousand Best Stories'*. There are four numbered sections – a practice more usual in much longer stories, and of these the first sets the scene and gives us a back story that takes us as far as that second marriage, and the elopement to the eponymous wood.

The other three tell the ongoing story and cover a much tighter period of time. The second introduces a new character, from whose perspective this third person tale is seen from now on, and who, visiting the country to find a suitable site for a rural retreat, bumps into his old friend Ackersley, who brings him to the house where the couple have fled. In the third section, which follows immediately from the second in both time and place, Ackersley, now calling himself Beckersley, tells him of all that has happened since the elopement. It is a story of paradise turned to hell, for the beautiful Nina, snubbed by an old acquaintance, has declined into alcoholism, has died, and is now buried in an unmarked grave 'in the heart of the wood' that surrounds the house. In the final section, the friend returns to the spot, to witness the burial of Beckersley, and is told what will become of the graves, the house, and the wood itself.

In many respects it is one of those over-emotional stories that we like to think a repressed society might wallow in to relieve itself, but there is something more to it than that, and I think that what that is lies in the telling.

To introduce a major character at such a late stage in a short story, fully one quarter of the way in, might seem a risky venture. It certainly changes the relationship between the reader and the story, and between the reader and the third person narrator. What had the ambience of a distant report now seems much more close-focus. We sit, along with the narrator on the shoulder of the new character, who appears at the opening of the second section without warning or preamble.

'Five years later it occurred to Algernon Gill...'

My first thought was, what have I missed? For Gill has not been referred to before, even obliquely. Seemingly entirely unconnected with the history that has gone before Gill catches his train out 'past Pinner........and on with a rush to Cheverley, on the Rickamnsworth line,' For a London readership this must have been the outer limits where strange tales of rural bliss, or horror, could be expected to unfold. It was, Lucy Lane Clifford has her narrator tell us, 'a quiet little station, that looked as if it had been dropped out of a dream.'

At the refreshment room in the station Gill takes a whisky and soda, and in walks Ackersley.

'...a vision of boyhood rose before his eyes,'

Ackersley is quick to tell Gill of his situation, and this, though back story to him progresses the story for us, and, fills the section.

'isolated little place, thirty acres, mostly wood,'

But Gill spots as soon as they get outside, that there is something wrong.

'"You are ill old chap."'

More than simply ill, Ackersley is not living a conventional life, any more than he had as an actor. He confesses he has 'half a dozen fellows' staying with him, but it is what they are that will shock Gill, and perhaps us.

'..a rummy set,.......God's leavings, as we are,'

As they drive to this strange house, Ackersley tells it all. The wealth, the marriage, the decline, the aftermath. He speaks of his need to clothe with theatricality the reality of his situation, a theme that runs through this story.

'life is sometimes too bare and grim to face unless it is decked with a few emotional effects.'

The wood has been fenced to keep out rabbits, and Beckersley, as he now calls himself, regrets that it keeps out also 'the tramp.'

'I shall make it up to him.' He promises.

The break to the next section signals a change in tone and mood, not one of time or place, and Gill is taken into the wood, to see the unmarked grave of Nina. It is like 'a Primeval forest' Gill observes.

Beckersley urges his one time friend to join him and the

crew at the house for a drinking bout, but Gill, horrified, flees back to London on his appointed train.

The fourth section has Gill again as our proxy in the story. He reluctantly attends Beckersley's funeral, at first refusing to accept the glass of champagne he is invited to take at the graveside.

> '"I feel sure," the doctor said deferentially to Gill, "it would hurt our friend if he could know that any of us refused to carry out his strange idea....'

Gill submits, and drinks. Then the housekeeper, one of the motley crew that Beckersley has 'saved,' puts a gift in the grave, and Gill watches as the hole is filled in and covered over, and we are left with that mournful legacy that I began with. Gill remains a reluctant witness to, rather than a willing participant in the events, and this helps to offset the inherent sentimentality of the story. Gill is keeping our feet on some sort of rational ground. One could find several such mournful, and one or two rather more up-beat but equally sentimental endings from within Hammerton's collection.

What is more remarkable than the sentiment however, is the language, for that is simple, direct, and pared down in a way that – despite the several other examples of such 'modern' writing that I have found from the period, her and elsewhere – I still find surprising from writers of this generation. I sometimes wonder if writers whose language doesn't seem to have aged were deliberately excluded from our canons of the past.

It's the structures of the sentences that give it these qualities of clarity and simplicity. They are constructed in that open form, that adds incrementally to what already makes sense, rather than those which increase the quantity of what is unintelligible until a key clause puts in a verb that will unlock the sense of the whole.

> 'Ackersley was a gentleman, had been in the Hussars – a crack regiment;but couldn't afford to keep it up, chucked it, and went on the stage.'

> 'She was a tall white faced girl of twenty, with a beautiful mouth, strange blue eyes, and quantities of dark hair with a crink in it.'

It's not necessarily the length of a sentence that makes it hard to understand. The organisation of the information, and the order in which we read it, is the greater help to understanding. And look too at the words used. None of them present difficulties of interpretation, even a century after they were written. The longest, most 'academic' or Latinate word I could find in the entire story was 'constitution,' though I don't guarantee not to have missed something!

Almost every sentence is constructed in this way. There are short sentences too, carrying one or two, simple images.

> 'But Gill caught the 6.20 train.'

> 'It was half-past when he reached Cheverley.'

> 'Liggin was there with his harp.'

Such sentences propel the story along in a clear, fast trajectory, without convolutions or conundrums. This is language for story, not for crossword puzzlers.

There is a Gothic quality to the tale, and an almost adolescent hysteria about Beckersley's reaction to his wife's death, but I suspect that it depicts the sort of events we have all fantasised about committing, if not actually put into practice. It's emotionalism may be more accurate than its psychology. Gill, with his observations and revulsions, allows us a screen of rational decency between ourselves and the story, but it is noticeable that Lucy Lane gives us the content of Beckersley's last wishes, rather than a comment of Gill's upon them, as the closing words; and they are words of compassion, inclusion, and charity towards the traveller and the outsider.

> '...the gypsy is to be allowed to pitch his tent if he chooses, and the tramp to find a shelter if he can.'

11 CAPTAIN KNOT
BY SIR ARTHUR QUILLER-COUCH

Sir Arthur Quiller-Couch (1863-1944), popularly known as Q, sometimes pinned his short stories to an historical event. *The Laird's Luck* hinges on an event that takes place on the eve of the Battle of Quatre Bras in the Waterloo campaign. *Lieutenant Lapenotiere* has as its eponymous hero the man who brings to the Admiralty the despatches telling of Nelson's death at Trafalgar. *Frenchman's Creek* retells an incident, whether alleged, historical or imaginary I am not sure, in the life of Captain Bligh of the Bounty. There may well be other examples of which I am not aware.

There is one story, however, pinned to a date, rather than an incident, which might be hard for the modern reader to take. First published in 1917, *Captain Knot* is set in a public house in Bristol on the evening of Saturday, 11th August, 1742.

If it were not for that specific reference, made early on in the story, the tale might have been set several decades before or after without requiring major or perhaps only one change, so far as I can tell. It is a story of three seamen conversing. They meet and talk about past events of their seafaring lives. The story is shot, to borrow a metaphor from that other storytelling means, the movie, over the shoulder of the eponymous Captain, which immediately raises the question of how we are to feel about him, as the main protagonist. Q may well be intending to wrong-foot us on this one.

As the story opens Q focuses on him:

> 'Aaron Knot, master of the Virginia barque *Jebioda*, though a member of the Society of Friends and a religious man by nature, had a tolerant and catholic mind, a quiet but insatiable curiosity in the ways of his fellow-men (seafarers and sinners especially), with a temperate zest for talking with strangers and listening to them.'

It's a long sentence, and gives us several key words to chew over, all of which are cast into doubt by that early 'though.' In a paragraph that takes up most of the first page of the story, Q adds to the description, telling us how Knot dresses – as a Quaker – and behaves – 'long hours, night after night, in his cabin, peaceably thinking about God' – and how old he is – 'sixty years.' His cargo is 'mainly' tobacco, which he has brought from Virginia. There is no mention yet, of what he might have carried on his homeward journey.

In the 'Welcome Home' tavern there are two men, seated in conversation, one older, the other younger, and Knot falls into conversation with them, thinking, as he does, that the older man is known to him from long ago. The penny, or should that be the doubloon, soon drops. The older man is a pirate, one of a crew that Knot has previously encountered, and whose fates will be revealed over the course of the story.

Q is a straightforward writer in many ways, but his simple, accessible language carries subtleties of meaning that raise questions we, rather than he, are to answer. That 'though' in the first sentence might be a good example of how Q works.

Knot's first exchanges are with the landlady, whose husband he enquires after. Knot's is a regular run, and the tavern, therefore, a regular haunt. The landlady explains that her husband 'is like every other fool in Bristol, crazy after the new preacher'. The preacher in question is John Wesley, and Knot comments that 'in Georgia (...) they did not think much of him.' This is the reference that pins the story to that particular date, and to the Weslyan mission of saving souls, and, by extension to the wider issue of what it means to be a Christian, or perhaps any other follower of a moral compass..

It is this comment that brings the younger of the two men, who is also a convert, into conversation with the captain, and soon after, Knot recognises the older man. Though the younger has said that he is in the business of 'The saving of souls,' and has cited that of his companion as being his current task – 'I know his need, and it's a bitter hard one' - as the conversation develops we find that the younger man has, in years gone by been a confederate of the pirate, and instrumental in helping him to evade arrest.

The tale tangles as we discover more about the three men. The pirate 'got the King's pardon for it these four years.' The younger man has been a looter of wrecks, and his father a man of 'free trade' – used in the story to signify smuggling.

Much of the conversation centres on the pirate's ship, The Rover, an almost bewitched ship, and one that eventually even the pirates themselves have to struggle to free themselves from when they become tired of their trade and want to retire to benefit from the loot they have amassed. Save for the man in the tavern, all the crew that are discussed have come to the slip-knotted end of a hangman's rope.

As the stories, and Q's story, come to an end, the last sighting of The Rover is told. This is where the story really jars with a modern reader, for within the space of three lines a word that it is almost impossible to use these days is drawn upon on three occasions. The ship, in which the pirate by then is 'honestly' serving, encounters The Rover, but it is being badly handled, its almost magical qualities of sea-worthiness no longer in evidence. Far from being afraid of it, the merchantman boards it.

'The hold was empty, but for nine niggers – live niggers...'

A skeleton crew is left to bring the ship in with the merchantman, but The Rover does not make it to port. 'She never was for port' Knot observes, to end the story.

Though the 'n' word has not been used previously in the story, the clue to its coming has been given. Earlier, as Knot gives his account of an encounter with The Rover, he has revealed the nature of his own seafaring.

'...the *Jebioda* standing for home with a hold full of negroes..'

There are two 'n' words, one descriptive, the other perjorative, and it's interesting that Q uses both, in the mouths of his characters, but not in the same mouth. Much of the discussion in the story, about The Rover, and about ships in general has been about whether or not they can be talked about as having souls, or characters.

> 'You're talking too deep for me, sir' said Williamson, rubbing his jaw. 'A ship with a soul, you say?'

> '...there's something belonging to her, and to her only,'

> 'I'm not denying as a ship may have a character,'

Perhaps this is why Q chose to pin his story to a Saturday evening in August 1742, when John Wesley was preaching near Bristol. Perhaps this is why his opening description of the Quaker, Knot, is subverted by that 'though'. Perhaps the souls and characters of ships and of men are being compared, and perhaps some of the latter too, and the eponymous Captain Knot among them, 'never was for port.'

12 BUILT UPON DECEIT
THE OLD MAN BY DAPHNE DU MAURIER

Daphne du Maurier has the reputation of being a writer of unsettling, even scary stories. Hitchcock's famous horror movie ***The Birds*** was based on her short story of the same name, and it's worth noting that he felt he had to tone down the ending. In the even creepier short story **Don't Look Now**, a recently bereaved father follows a childlike figure through the back alleyways of Venice, only to find himself confronting a murderous, psychopathic dwarf.

There's something odd too about *The Old Man*, and you don't have to be expecting oddity to notice it. In the story, the first person narrator responds to a curious holidaymaker who is visiting his part of the coast. The story begins:

> 'Did I hear you asking about the Old Man? I thought so. You're a newcomer to the district, here on holiday … It's a lovely spot isn't it? Quiet and remote.

You can't wonder at the old man choosing to live here.'

Hints and clues throughout the story make us as wary of the eponymous hero – the Old Man – just as the narrator is wary, but neither the narrator nor the person who has warned him about 'the old man' gives the game away, at least not to begin.

'I had the feeling, from the very first, that he had done something, or something had been done to him, that gave him a grudge against the world.'

We keep a safe distance away from the Old Man, along with the narrator, who carries a big stick, just in case. It is easy to believe that the old man is to be avoided, because we mistake what the narrator *tells* us for something that has actually happened: 'I had been warned about him … give the old man who lived down by the lake a wide berth.'

This is a strange place to choose to live – 'exposed to all the weather' – and we soon observe the strange behaviour of this seemingly dysfunctional family who are neighbours to the narrator – behaviour that moves through odd, to threatening, to murderous. 'It's about the family I really wanted to tell you. Because there was a tragedy, you see.' That tragedy is the murder of the son by the Old Man, and when we realise this it's fair to wonder how come the Old Man is still living at liberty by the lake.

By this time, we begin to question some of the oddity in the story. Even the narrator – or at least his guarded response to what we think he is telling us he has seen – appears to be a little odd: 'I suppose I could have told someone, but … They might have taken the old man away.'

Eventually, we are let in on the secret, and see that we have been misled, perhaps even that we have misled ourselves: '…suddenly I saw the old man stretch his neck and beat his wings.'

'The Old Man' is a story built upon a simple deception: a metaphor that has been extended as far as a swan's neck is long. The 'old man' is the nickname given to the male swan in a family of swans nesting, quite un-oddly, by the lake, and behaving in a way that, for swans, is not at all dysfunctional. The deception begins with the title itself, and deepens with our introduction to the family: '…he was living here beside the lake, along of his missus.' But the clues are there, in the oddities of the story, its events, and its narration.

'The Old Man' might be thought to have too much of an O. Henry trick-ending, though the trick here, like many good tricks, has taken place right at the beginning. You might wonder though, once we've found out that the old man is a swan, what reason is there to read the story again? Even on a first reading, I confess, I felt cheated, as well as fooled. Yet there was, in that 'fooling', some sort of revelation about myself that I had not expected to encounter. C.S.Lewis, in **_Of Other Worlds_**, wrote of the 'surprisingness' of story – rather than an *actual surprise* – as being what draws us back for subsequent readings. It's undoubtedly true, too, that our favourite stories, the ones we read or listen to again and again, are not the ones we have forgotten, but the ones we have not.

The element we may remember from this story is not that we were tricked by it, but that we were *uncomfortable* during the reading. We knew that something was not quite right – with the events being described, and with the narrator's reaction, and actions, in response to them.

> 'I shouted across to the old man, 'You murderer, you bloody goddamned murderer'. You'll want to know what I did. I went back and got a spade and I dug a grave…'

The weakness of the trick ending might be that, like the one-shot pistol, once it has gone off it cannot be fired again. Yet, on re-reading, the knowledge that we're being fooled makes us look for the places in which that fooling was taking place – the sentences, the phrases, the individual words: 'missus', 'son', 'mother'. Yet words are adroitly avoided. 'Home' is used, and it is even described as a 'Funny sort of lash-up … exposed to all the weather', but the word 'house' is not to be seen.

> 'There was the old man, outside his home, staring down towards his son with murder in his eyes … I bet that old fellow is one hell of a character.'

This is a story about how and, perhaps, why we can be, were, and will be fooled, not only in short stories, but in real life. It is a story about language, and how we use it, and how we can misunderstand it. It is a story about contexts, and assumptions, and prejudices; about the very great difference, to which our attention must surely have been drawn, between how we feel about a dysfunctional swan family, and a dysfunctional human one. Now that's a good reason to read a story for the first, second, and subsequent times.

THE SILENT LIFE WITHIN

ABOUT THE AUTHOR

Mike Smith has published poetry, short plays and essays. His plays are available through Lazy Bee Scripts. He regularly writes for Thresholds, the International Post Graduate Short Story Forum. Writing as Brindley Hallam Dennis he has published several collections of short stories and a novella. His work has been widely performed and published in magazines, journals and anthologies. He lives in north Cumbria within sight of three mountain tops and a sliver of Solway Firth. He blogs at www.Bhdandme.wordpress.com

The Broken Mirror (poetry)
No Easy Place (poetry)
Valanga (poetry)
Martin? Extinct? (poetry)
English of the English (essays on A.E.Coppard)
Readings for Writers vol.1
The Poetic Image (a short course in the short story)
Love and Nothing Else (Readings for Writers vol.2)
An Early Frost (poetry)

As Brindley Hallam Dennis
Second Time Around (short stories)
A Penny Spitfire (novella)
Talking To Owls (short stories)
Departures (short stories)
Ambiguous Encounters (short stories with Marilyn Messenger)
Ten Murderous Tales (short stories)
The Man Who Found A Barrel Full of Beer (short stories)

Made in the USA
Charleston, SC
03 September 2016